D1247408

SUPERMAN CREATED BY
JERRY SIEGEL AND JOE SHUSTER
BY SPECIAL ARRANGEMENT WITH
THE JERRY SIEGEL FAMILY

STONE ARCH BOOKS
a capstone imprint

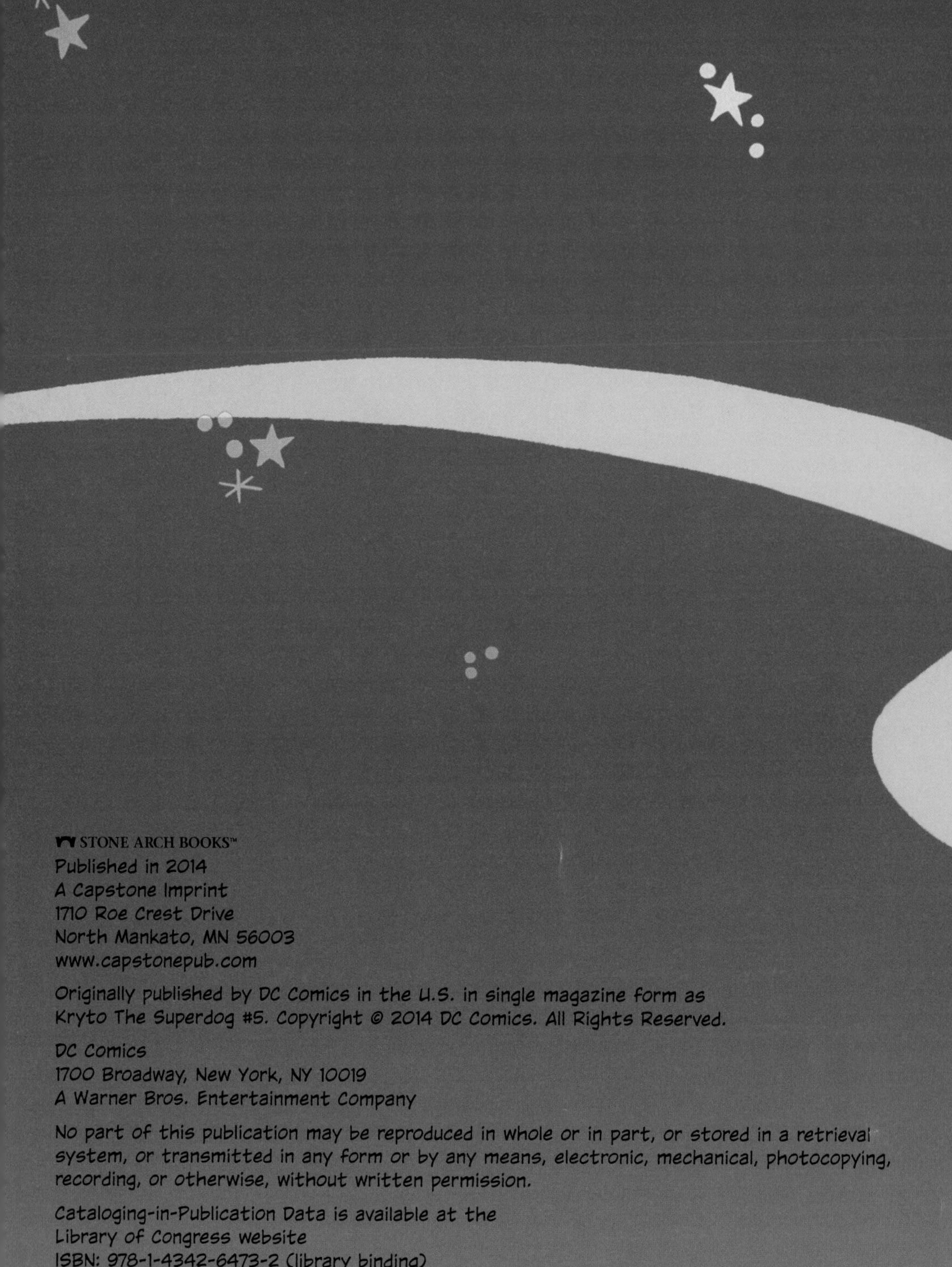

STONE ARCH BOOKS™
Published in 2014
A Capstone Imprint
1710 Roe Crest Drive
North Mankato, MN 56003
www.capstonepub.com

DC Comics
1700 Broadway, New York, NY 10019
A Warner Bros. Entertainment Company

Cataloging-in-Publication Data is available at the
Library of Congress website
ISBN: 978-1-4342-6473-2 (library binding)

Summary: Heel before Dom! Krypto discovers he's not the Last Pup of Krypton after all--and Dom is not a good dog!

STONE ARCH BOOKS
Ashley C. Andersen Zantop Publisher
Michael Dahl Editorial Director
Donald Lemke & Sean Tulien Editors
Bob Lentz Art Director
Hilary Wacholz Designer

DC COMICS
Kristy Quinn Original U.S. Editor

Printed in China by Nordica.
1013 / CA21301918
092013 007744NORDS14

KRYPTO
The SUPERDOG™

Three Naughty Doggies!

JESSE LEON MCCANN..................................WRITER
SCOTT COHN..PENCILLER
AL NICKERSON...INKER
DAVE TANGUAY.......................................COLORIST
DAVE TANGUAY....................................... LETTERER

PLEASE TELL US ANOTHER STORY, UNCLE STREAKY!
NAH, SORRY, KIDS. HAVE IMPORTANT SUPERHERO DUTIES TO ATTEND TO.
OH, PLEEEEASE!
PLEASE! PLEASE! PLEASE!
WELL, I GUESS I COULD TELL ONE MORE. THIS IS THE TALE THAT I CALL . . .
THREE NAUGHTY DOGGIES!
A LONG TIME AGO, WHEN SUPERDOG WAS JUST A LITTLE PUP, HE LIVED FAR, FAR AWAY, ON A PLANET CALLED KRYPTON. HE LIVED WITH HIS BOY KAL-EL, WHOSE FATHER WAS A FAMOUS SCIENTIST NAMED ...
JOR-EL!
JESSE LEON MCCANN – WRITER
SCOTT COHN – PENCILLER
AL NICKERSON – INKER
DAVE TANGUAY – LETTERER/COLORIST
RACHEL GLUCKSTERN – ASSOC. EDITOR
JOAN HILTY – EDITOR

JOR-EL! THE HIGH COUNCIL IS VERY CONCERNED!
MY FRIEND, THE KRYPTONIAN HIGH COUNCIL IS ALWAYS CONCERNED ABOUT SOMETHING. WHAT IS IT THIS TIME?

RECENTLY, YOU SENT GENERAL ZOD AND ACCOMPLICES INTO EXILE IN THE PHANTOM ZONE.
YES, THEY WERE VICIOUS CRIMINALS.
WELL, GENERAL ZOD HA LEFT US SOME... PROBLEMS.
WHAT DO YOU MEAN?

ZOD LEFT US HIS THREE NAUGHTY DOGGIES.
WHATEVER SHALL WE DO WITH THEM?
DOM
VILEA
TRONK
GROWL!
SNARL!
SNAP!

"IT DIDN'T TAKE LONG FOR JOR-EL TO COME UP WITH A SOLUTION...
THE MATTER IS EASILY SOLVED, MY FRIEND, FOR I SHALL SEND THESE THREE VICIOUS CANINES TO A PLANET THAT ENCIRCLES SIRIUS, THE DOG STAR.
SIRIUS?
SSSSSSSS!
GRRRRRR!
COMPLETELY. THERE THEY SHAL LIVE AMONG THEI OWN KIND.

GRRRRRRR! HOW DARE THE HAIRLESS ONES SEND US AWAY!
SHRED!
TEAR!
RIP!
SHVOOOM!
WARNING! WARNING! TAMPERING WITH THE SHIP'S WIRING IS NOT ADVISED.

"TOO BAD THE DOGS WRECK THE ROCKET'S ANTI-METE DEVICE, BECAUSE A METE STRUCK THE SHIP AND THRE THEM FAR OFF COURSE ..

HIBERNATION GAS RELEASED. SLEEP TIGHT!
WHAT?! NOOOOOO!
PSSSSSSS!

"MANY YEARS PASSED, AND THE SHIP LANDED ON EARTH ...
SO ***THIS*** IS THE PLANET OF THE DOG STAR? IT'S NOT SO BAD.
YES, VILEA. THE YELLOW RAYS OF THIS PLANET'S SUN MAKE ME FEEL ***VITAL*** AND ***STRONG***. IT'S AS IF I COULD ...

...FLY!
WE ***ALL*** CAN!
HRRRK!
WHOOOSH!

AND LOOK! WE HAVE ***REMARKABLE STRENGTH***, AS WELL!
EXCELLENT! PERHAPS OUR POWERS ARE ***GREATER*** THAN THE INHABITANTS OF THIS PLANET.
ARRRRR!
WHOOOSH!
CLUMP

IF SO, WE MAY ***SUCCEED*** WHERE GENERAL ZOD FAILED, AND ***CONQUER*** AN ***ENTIRE PLANET!*** THEN I, ***DOM***, SHALL BE ***RULER***!

"THAT'S WHERE ***I*** COME INTO THE STORY. I WAS HAVING A ***FEAST*** FIT FOR A KING. MAN! YOU WOULD NOT ***BELIEVE*** ALL THE GREAT THINGS TO EAT, JUST LYING AROUND ON THE GROUND AT A ***TRAVELING CARNIVAL***!

CORN DOGS

"LITTLE DID I KNOW MY MEAL WAS ABOUT TO BE ***INTERRUPTED***!"

VILEA, TRONK—CREATE SOME HAVOC, AND WE'LL SEE WHAT SORT OF HEROES THIS PLANET HAS TO CHALLENGE US.
HEEEEY!
GRRRRR!
POPCORN
BUMP!
CRASH!

SOMEBODY NEEDS TO TEACH THOSE NAUGHTY DOGGIES SOME MANNERS. SOMEBODY LIKE SUPERCAT!
LIGHTS! STREAKY! ACTION!
PUH-TUH! PUH-TUH-PUH-TA!
PING! PING! PEW!

HEY, GUYS, I HATE TO BREAK IT TO YOU, BUT PLAYTIME IS OVER. TIME TO TURN-TAIL AND RUN.
THIS BUMPKIN IS THE BEST THEY HAVE TO OFFER?

HAVEN'T YOU HEARD OF ME? I'M SUPERCAT, THE CAT OF STEEL!
NOW, UNLESS YOU W
ME TO DROP YOU
YOUR CABOO
YOU'LL VAMOO

WHAT AN ANNOYING CREATURE. I'D BE DELIGHTED TO CRUSH IT FOR YOU.
HOLD ON, HEH HEH! LET'S NOT BE HASTY! MAYBE WE SHOULD TALK THIS OVER.
JUST REMOVE IT FROM OUR SIGHT, VILEA.

MY PLEASURE!
WHOA! WHOA! WHOA! HOLD ON, LADY, THIS AIN'T GOOD FOR MY DIGESTION!
WHIR!
WHIR!
WHIR!
WHIR!

EEEEEEEEK!
ZZZZIIIP!
OW! HOO-BOY! I THINK SHE JUST DENTED MY SELF-ESTEEM.
CLANG!
EVERYTHING'S OKAY! SORRY ABOUT THE INCONVENIENCE, OLKS! I WILL NOW RETURN YOUR SEATS TO THEIR UPRIGHT AND LOCKED POSITION!
RRRRONNG!
EE-EE-EE-EE!
YOU CAUGHT ME WHEN I WASN'T LOOKING! NOW, HOW BOUT A TASTE OF MY HEAT VISION?
VILEA, THE TIRESOME FELINE HAS RETURNED. GET RID OF IT, ONCE AND FOR ALL.
CH! A RICOCHET-BEAM, RNT BOTTOM ATTACK! HOW SNEAKY CAN YA GET?
BWOSH!
FWOOOOOSH!
ZZZZAP!
, OL' UNCLE AKY WOULD R FLY FROM IR FIGHT. I DIDN'T T TO EM-RASS THEM EATING THEM BY MYSELF!
WHOOSH!
I'D BETTER GO GET HELP FROM MY BUDDY KRYPTO!
"IT JUST SO HAPPENED THAT KRYPTO AND HIS FAMILY WERE HALFWAY AROUND THE WORLD ..."
TAHITI IS GREAT, EH, BOY?
YOU BET, KEVIN! IT'S NICE TO GET AWAY FROM THE CHALLENGES SUPERDOG FACES EVERY DAY! AT LEAST FOR A LITTLE WHILE.

AH!
HIYA, GUYS!
STREAK
WHAT ARE
DOING HER

COME OVER HERE! I'VE GOT SOMETHING TO SHOW YOU.
WHY? IS THERE TROUBLE IN METROPOLIS?
UH... NOT ANYMORE.

YOU MIGHT SAY TROUBLE FOLLOWED ME HERE.
YOU! I REMEMBER YOU!
AND I REMEMBER YOU— THE WHELP THAT BELONGED TO JOR-EL.
HOW FORTUNATE. YOU AND YOUR NEW WORLD WILL BOW DOWN TO ME.

WHO ARE THEY, BOY?
JUST SOME BAD DOGS I THOUGHT I'D NEVER SEE AGAIN.
THIS IS YOUR
HAIRLESS ONE?
PERHAPS AFTER I'
DEFEATED YOU, I
MAKE HIM MY
PET.

KEVIN! RUN BACK TO THE BUNGALOW AND TAKE YOUR FAMILY INSIDE. I HAVE A FEELING THINGS ARE GOING TO GET ROUGH OUT HERE!
BECAUSE GETTING RID OF NAUGHTY DOGGIES LOOKS LIKE A JOB...
WHRRRRR!

...FOR KRYPTO THE SUPERDOG
SPECIAL EFFECT
AND CAPES. HO
QUAINT.
THAT'S WHAT I'M TALKIN' BOUT!

, HOW HANDSOME YOU ARE IN YOUR AK AND KRYPTONIAN BLEM. I LOVE A DOG IN UNIFORM.
WELL,...ER,... GULP...GEE, THANKS!

HERE, GOOD-LOOKING, I THINK YOU'LL GET A KICK OUT OF THIS!
OOH! THAT'LL LEAVE A BRUISE!
PUNT!
OOF!

WHAP! SNAP! WHAP! SNAP! WHAP! SNAP!
YIP! DIDN'T SEE THAT COMING!

M! DAD! WE HAVE TO GET INSIDE! A BIG...MONSOON IS COMING THIS WAY!
MONSOON? BUT IT'S A CLEAR, BEAUTIFUL DAY!
HA! KWYPTO PLAY WIF BLACK DOGGIES. HA HA!

YOU'VE OVERSTAYED YOUR WELCOME ON THIS ISLAND. HERE'S SOMETHING TO GET YOU GOING!
AHHHHH!
FWSSSSSSSSH!
CLONK!
IT BLOWS YOUR MIND, DOESN'T IT?

WSSSSSSH!
UH... M-MAYBE YOU'RE RIGHT, SON. LET GET UNDERCOVER!
OH, DEAR! WHERE'S KRYPTO?
HE'LL BE ALL RIGHT... I HOPE.

"THAT'S WHEN THE BATTLE GOT **HOT AND HEAVY**! AND, EVEN THOUGH WE WERE OUTNUMBERED THREE-TO-TWO, SUPERDOG AND I HELD OUR OWN...
EE-EE-EE-EE!
BLAK!
EE-EE-PISH!
ZZZZAP!
YEEOWCH! TWICE IN ONE DAY! I HOPE THE FELLAS BACK HOME DON'T HEAR ABOUT THIS!

"I COUNTERED WITH MY PATENTED **CAT BOX** MANEUVER ...
SKRITCH! SKR
SKRITCHY-SKR
HERE
SAND IN
EYE

"THEN DOM **THREW** THE CLOSEST THING HE COULD FIND AT US—**TRONK!**"
OOF
BAMFF!!
HAW!
BONK!

KER-SMASH
SPAA-LURR!!
SSSSSSS!

DIDN'T YOUR **MOM** EVER TEACH YOU TO **PLAY NICE**?
LET'S JUST WIPE THAT **DIRTY LOOK** OFF YOUR FACE!
WAIT! GLUB, GLUB! MY BEAUTIFUL **FUR**!

ITS LI
ALWAYS
YOU **CAN'T B**
THE **STREAK**, 'C
THE **STREAK C**
BE **B**
GIVE IT **UP**, DOM. IT'S **TWO** AGAINST **ONE**, NOW.
CLUNK!
SLOSH!

ERE'S HE G? IS HE OWING IN TOWEL?
I WOULDN'T BET ON IT!
KEVIN, GET BACK UNDER HERE UNTIL WE KNOW IT'S SAFE.
OOOH! KOOKY NUT! HA-HA!
I-I THINK IT'S OKAY.

FWHOOSH!
HEY!

UT ME OWN!
NOW BOW DOWN TO ME, PET OF JOR-EL, OR THIS HAIRLESS ONE WILL DRAW HIS LAST BREATH!

SAY THE WORD, K-DOG, AND I'LL RIP THIS BULLY LIMB FROM LIMB!
NO! EVERYONE CALM DOWN.
ALL RIGHT, DOM, I SURRENDER. WAIT HERE WHILE I GET MY CROWN AND OTHER CEREMONIAL ITEMS WE'LL NEED FOR THE TRANSFER OF POWER.

SUPERDOG RETURNED A SHORT WHILE ATER WITH A CASE THAT HE SAID HAD A CROWN IN IT. HE TOLD US TO GO ALONG WITH THE CEREMONY..."
I WILL NOW CROWN YOU DOM THE FIRST, EMPEROR OF THE WHOLE PLANET!
AT LAST! IT IS A GLORIOUS DAY.

ARGHH! WHA-WHATS HAPPENING TO US?
IT'S CALLED KRYPTONITE, AND YOU PUPPIES HAVE BEEN PUNK'D!
I BORROWED IT FROM SUPERMAN'S FORTRESS OF SOLITUDE.
ROH!
I FEEL SO WEAK!

THIS LEAD-LINED MAT
WILL PROTECT US FROM T
KRYPTONITE INSIDE.
COME ON, STREAKY, LET'S FIND THE ROCKET THESE THREE CAME IN. RUFF, RUFF AND AWAY!
HURRY BACK, BOY!
MOA

"BACK IN METROPOLIS, IT DIDN'T TAKE US LONG TO FIND THE ROCKET...
HEY! WHY DON'T WE BURY THIS IN MY BACKYARD, SO I COULD HAVE A ROCKET PLAYHOUSE TOO?
NO, WE NEED THE ROCKET TO SEND THESE VILLAINS AWAY.
BUT TO WHERE? MAYBE THERE'S A CLUE ON THE INSIDE.
GREETINGS! THIS SHIP WAS MEANT TO LAND NEAR SIRIUS, THE DOG STAR. UNFORTUNATELY, IT LANDED ON EARTH, INSTEAD.
I WILL NOW INSTRUCT YOU ON HOW TO REPROGRAM THE SHIP'S ONBOARD COMPUTER.
HOLY MACARONI! NICE TV PICTURE!
IT'S A HOLOGRAM RECORDING, STREAKY.
"SUPERDOG RESET THE ROCKET'S CONTROLS, AND THAT WAS THE LAST WE SAW OF THE THREE NAUGHTY DOGGIES.
SHVOOOM!
MANY YEARS FROM NOW, THEY'LL LAND ON A PLANET IN THE SIRIUS SYSTEM, WHERE EVERYONE HAS TO ACT SERIOUS ALL THE TIME AND THE
NEVER HAVE ANY FUN. THE END!
"SIRIUS" ISN'T SPELT THE SAME AS "SERIOUS." YOU MADE THAT UP, UNCLE STREAKY!
TELL US ANOTHER STORY! PLEASE!
PLEASE! PLEASE! PLEASE!
"SIGH!" THE PRICE OF BEING A SUPERHERO IS
HIGH. BUT SOMEBODY'S
GOT TO DO IT!

AH! CONNECTICUT IN THE FALL...
BEAUTIFUL LAKES, BLUE SKY, LEAVES OF A THOUSAND COLORS, AND...
...BATS!
SHOO! GET AWAY!
SKREEE! SKREE!
THAT'S NOT BATS!
JESSE LEON MCCANN – WRITER
MIN S. KU – PENCILLER
JEFF ALBRECHT – INKER
VE TANGUAY – LETTERER/COLORIST
ACHEL GLUCKSTERN-ASST. EDITOR
JOAN HILTY– EDITOR

E BATCAVE ON THE OUTSKIRTS OF GOTHAM CITY...
ARE YOU SURE BATMAN WON'T MIND YOU SHOWING ME AROUND?
HEY, HE'S MY PARTNER. HIS CASA IS MI DOG CASA.

...SUDDENLY, THERE WERE A THOUSAND BATS ALL AROUND ME!

THEY TOOK MY GRANDPA'S **GOLD** POCKET WATCH AND MADE ME LOSE MY **FAVORITE** FISHING POLE!
ANYONE **ELSE** HAVE A RUN-IN WITH THESE THIEVING BATS?

"YES, THERE WERE A NUMBER OF INCIDENTS...
SKREEE!
SKREEE!
SKREEE!
HEY!
"...THEY SWARMED THROUGH TOWN, STEALING **EVERYTHING** IN THEIR PATH.

"THEY ROBBED THE BANK, AND MADE OFF WITH SEVERAL THOUSAND **DOLLARS**.
SKREEE!

"THE JEWELRY STORE OWNER BLEW A **GASKET** AND ENDED UP IN THE **HOSPITAL**."
SKREEE!
SKREEE!

ALL RIGHT, JIM. **I'LL** LOOK INTO IT.
THANKS, BATMAN. I'D STICK AROUND AND HELP, BUT I'M DUE BACK IN GOTHAM CITY.

END TRANSMISSION.
HMM... JIM GORDON JUST **HAPPENS** TO BE IN A TOWN WHEN THERE'S A **BAT** ATTACK. **COINCIDENCE**? OR IS SOMEONE JUST TRYING TO GET MY **ATTENTION**?
I NEED YOUR **HELP** ON THIS ONE, BOYS.

ER IN CONNECTICUT...
HA HA HA! YOU LOOK SILLY, MOO COW!

HEY, BUD! STOP MESSING WITH THE HIRED HELP! THE BOSS IS CALLIN'!
NYAH-NYAH-NYAH!
CONNECTING

HO, HO, BOYS! WONDERFUL REPORT! HA HA HA HA HA!
BAT ATTACK HUGE SUCC

JUST KEEP BATMAN BUSY WHEN HE GETS THERE! IN FACT, HEE HEE, DRIVE HIM BATTY! HA HA HA HA!
I'M OUTTA HERE!

TOMORROW, 'LL HAVE BATMAN YING "RING AROUND HE BELFRIES"!
HA HA HA HA HA HA HA HA!
OST MISSION
SKREEE!
SKREEE!
SKREEE!
STAMP & CO
OH, NO! NOT AGAIN!

HAW! HOW DO YOU LIKE THAT, BUD? LOOT DELIVERED TO ORDER!
SKREEE!
SKREEE!
SKREEE!
YEAH, LOU, AND BEST OF ALL IT'S FREE. HA HA HA HA!

DON'T START COUNTING YOUR ILL-GOTTEN GAINS YET.
YIKES! IT'S BATMAN!
HE GOT HERE QUICK!

RUN, BUD, BEFORE OUR SPREE IS SPRUNG!
I'M RUNNIN', LOU, I'M RUNNIN'!

THEY FELL FOR IT!
IT TOOK EVERY FIBER OF MY BEING NOT TO BUST THOSE CROOKED CLOWNS.
REMEMBER: EVERYONE HERE NEEDS TO THINK BATMAN IS ON THE JOB.

I'M GLAD WE WERE ABLE TO FIND ALL THE TOWNSPEOPLE'S VALUABLES!
QUIET. WE DON'T WANT THEM TO THINK "BATMAN" HAS A SPLIT PERSONALITY.
HOORAY! THANK YOU, BATMAN!
MP & COIN

EXCELLENT JOB, BOYS! A BUSY BAT IS THE JOKER'S PLAYTHING. HO HO HA HA HA!

MEANWHILE...
THIS IS THE KIND OF PLACE WHERE BATS HANG AROUND. LET'S CHECK IT OUT!
RIGHT BEHIND YOU!

WHY DO TS LIVE IN CH GRIM PLACES?
HEY, DON'T KNOCK IT 'TIL YOU'VE TRIED IT.
SQUEEAK!
CREEAK!

HERE ARE SOME LIKELY SUSPECTS. NOW ALL WE NEED TO DO IS GET UP THERE AND ASK SOME QUESTIONS.
NOT A PROBLEM.

HEY, WAKE UP! WHAT DO YOU KNOW ABOUT ALL THESE THIEVING BATS?
AW, CAN'T YA SEE I GOT A TERRIBLE HEADACHE? KEEP YOUR VOICE DOWN!

DON'T MAKE ME COME UP THERE.
EEK! IT'S BAT-HOUND FROM GOTHAM CITY!
WE DIDN'T STEAL NOTHIN', I SWEAR! IT MUSTA BEEN THEM OUT-OF-TOWN BATS I SAW NEAR THE COW FIELDS!

THE NEXT AFTERNOON...
SKREEE!
SKREEE!
SKREEE!
JI-DANG'S SHOP
CHOE-CHOP CAFE
THE WEASELY BAT WAS RIGHT. THE SWARM IS HEADING FOR THE PASTURES OUTSIDE OF TOWN.
SNICKER! SNORT! BATMAN TOOK THE BAIT AGAIN!
THE BATMOBILE'S RAD
TRACKING IS ONLINE
WORKING PERFECTLY
SUPERDOG.
IT SHOULD LEAD US RIGHT TO THE BATS' HIDEOUT.

THAT'S GREAT, ACE!
WAIT. STOP HERE, SUPERDOG. THE BATS HAVE LANDED.

WELL, THERE'S THE LOOT, BUT I DON'T SEE WHERE THE BATS WENT.
I DON'T GET IT. HOW COULD THEY JUST DISAPPEAR LIKE THAT?

ATER THAT NIGHT...
SKREEE!
SKREEE!
TELL ME WHY WE'RE DOING THIS AGAIN, LOU?
I KNOW OUR MISSION IS TO KEEP BATMAN BUSY, BUT IF WE CAN KEEP SOME LOOT, TOO, IT'S JUST ICING ON THE CAKE. HA HA HA HA!
I LIKE CAKE, LOU! HA HA HA!

EEP LAUGHING, LOWLIFES. R CHUCKLES ARE ABOUT TO MEET MY KNUCKLES.
SWING!
AY YI YI! IT'S BATMAN!

HEY, BUD! WATCH WHERE YOU'RE GOIN'!
I TOLD YOU THE BLINDERS WERE A BAD IDEA, LOU!
RVE!

WHAT ARE YOU DOIN', BUD?!
I'M RIDIN' WITH YOU, LOU!
THEN WHO'S DRIVIN'?
AIIIEEEEE!

IMPRESSIVE... IN A DIMWITTED HYENA SORT OF WAY.
CRASH!

I CAN'T BELIEVE IT! THE BATS HAVE *DISAPPEARED* AGAIN.
RUN, BUD, RUN!

SHOULD I *ROUND UP* BUD AND LOU FOR QUESTIONING?

SOON...
HEY, *LOOK*, BUD! OUR BATS HAVE BEEN *WORKING OVERTIME* AND LEFT US A *PRESENT*!
THAT'S GREAT, LOU! NOW WE CAN BUY *ALL THE CAKE* WE WANT.

WE'RE *TRAPPED*, LOU! OUR CAKES ARE *COOKED*!
SPROING!
COOL IT WITH THE *CAKE THING*, BUD.

TIME FOR US TO HAVE A LONG OVERDUE *CHAT*, BOYS.

I DON'T CARE IF IT TAKES *ALL NIGHT*, YOU'RE GOING TO GIVE ME SOME ANSWERS.

OH NO! *ALL NIGHT*? YOU HEAR THAT,
LOUD AND *CLEAR*, BUD. AND I'M SENDING *THE BOSS* THE MESSAGE.

HA HA HA HA HA!
THAT'S GREAT! WE'VE GOT YOU JUST WHERE WE WANT YOU, BATMAN!
THERE'S ONLY ONE PROBLEM...

BATMAN IS MY PARTNER. I'M BAT-HOUND!
EE-HEE-HEE-HEE! MOOOO!

GASP!
I GOTTA TEXT THE BOSS! BATMAN IS ON TO HIM!

I DON'T
INK SO! I'LL
AKE THAT.
FINE! OUR BATS WILL STEAL ME ANOTHER ONE. HAW!

I HATE TO BREAK IT TO YOU, BUT WE FOUND YOUR BATS, HIDING RIGHT HERE IN PLAIN SIGHT.

YOU COULD MAKE THEM DO YOUR BIDDING BECAUSE THEY'RE NOT BATS AT ALL, THEY'RE ROBOTS.
SOON TO BE DEACTIVATED ROBOTS. LOOKS LIKE THE JOKER'S PLANS ARE JUST ABOUT WASHED UP!

MEANWHILE, IN GOTHAM CITY...
HA HA HA HEE HOO HOO! WITH BATMAN OTHERWISE OCCUPIED IN CONNECTICUT, THIS CAPER IS GOING TO BE A WALK IN THE PARK! WOO HOO HOO!
SOCK!
BIFF!
POW!
HURT!
PUNT!
HEY, WHAT'S GOING ON UP THERE? HALLOO? YOU BETTER NOT BE CLOWNING AROUND!
THAT'S MY JOB! HEE!
AND MY JOB IS TO MAKE SURE YOU'RE LOCKED UP TIGHT!
HSSS!
B-BUT...HOW DID YOU GET BACK TO GOTHAM CITY SO FAST?
I NEVER LEFT.
WELL DONE, EVERYONE! TWO CRIMES SOLVED IN ONE FELL SWOOP.
FROM NOW ON, ALL WE'LL HEAR FROM THESE CROOKS IS CANNED LAUGHS!
ARKHAM ASYLUM
GOTHAM

Superdog Jokes!

WHAT KIND OF DOG SPECIALIZES IN PRIZE FIGHTS?

A BOXER!

WHAT DO YOU CALL A CUTE RETRIEVER

LABRADOR-ABLE!

WHAT HAPPENS WHEN KRYPTO FIGHTS SNOOKY WOOKUMS?

FUR FLIES!

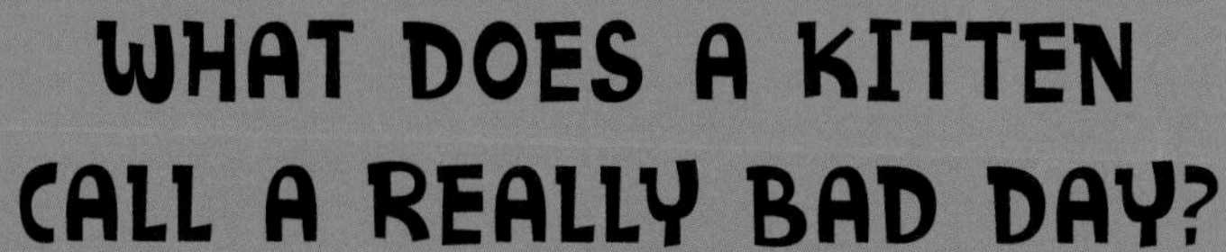

WHAT DOES A KITTEN CALL A REALLY BAD DAY?

A CAT-TASTROPHE!

JESSE LEON MCCANN WRITER

Jesse Leon McCann is a *New York Times* Top-Ten Children's Book Writer, as well as a prolific all-ages comics writer. His credits include Pinky and the Brain, Animaniacs, and Looney Tunes for DC Comics; Scooby-Doo and Shrek 2 for Scholastic; and The Simpsons and Futurama for Bongo Comics. He lives in Los Angeles with his wife and four cats.

SCOTT COHN PENCILLER

Scott Cohn is an experienced illustrator who has worked with clients like DC Comics, WWE, Harper Collins, Mirage, Dynamite, MTV, HBO, A&E, and Time Inc. just to name a few.

AL NICKERSON INKER

Al Nickerson has done illustration work for DC Comics, Archie, and Marvel.

DAVE TANGUAY COLORIST/LETTERER

David Tanguay has over 20 years of experience in the comic book industry. He has worked as an editor, layout artist, colorist, and letterer. He has also done web design, and he taught computer graphics at the State University of New York.

ACCOMPLICE (uh-KOM-pliss) – someone who helps another person commit a crime

CONQUER (KONG-kur) – to defeat and take control of an enemy

DEACTIVATED (dee-AK-ti-vay-tid) – turned off or disabled

EXILE (EG-zile) – to send someone away from their home

HASTY (HAY-stee) – too quick or hurried

HAVOC (HAV-uhk) – great damage and chaos

INHABITANTS (in-HAB-it-tuhnts) – people or animals that live in a certain place

MONSOON (mon-SOON) – a very strong wind that blows from the ocean toward land that brings heavy rains

SUSPECTS (SUHSS-spekts) – individuals thought to be guilty of a crime

Visual Questions & Prompt

1. BASED ON WHAT YOU KNOW FROM THIS STORY, WHY IS IT IMPORTANT FOR KRYPTO AND ACE TO MAKE EVERYONE THINK THAT BATMAN IS THE ONE WHO HELPED THEM?

2. IN THIS PANEL, THE MAN IN PURPLE IS REFERRING TO THE STAR, SIRIUS, BUT IT'S ALSO A PLAY ON WORDS, OR A PUN. WHAT IS THE SECOND MEANING OF HIS RESPONSE?

"IT DIDN'T TAKE LONG FOR JOR-EL TO COME UP WITH A SOLUTION...
THE MATTER IS EASILY SOLVED, MY FRIEND, FOR I SHALL SEND THESE THREE VICIOUS CANINES TO A PLANET THAT ENCIRCLES SIRIUS, THE DOG STAR.
SIRIUS?
2

IF YOU COULD CREATE A PACK OF ROBOTIC ANIMALS, WHAT
D WOULD YOU MAKE AND WHAT WOULD YOU DO WITH THEM?

BETWEEN THESE PANELS, WHY DO YOU THINK THE CREATORS MADE A PANEL BORDER WITH
BATS? HOW DOES IT AFFECT THE WAY YOU READ IT? HOW DOES IT MAKE YOU FEEL?

TOMORROW, WE'LL HAVE ***BATMAN*** PLAYING "RING AROUND THE ***BELFRIES***"!
HA HA HA HA HA HA HA HA!
LOST TRANSMISSION
SKREEE!
SKREEE!
SKREEE!
STAMP & COI
OH, NO! NOT AGAIN!
4

READ THEM ALL!

only from...

STONE ARCH BOOKS™

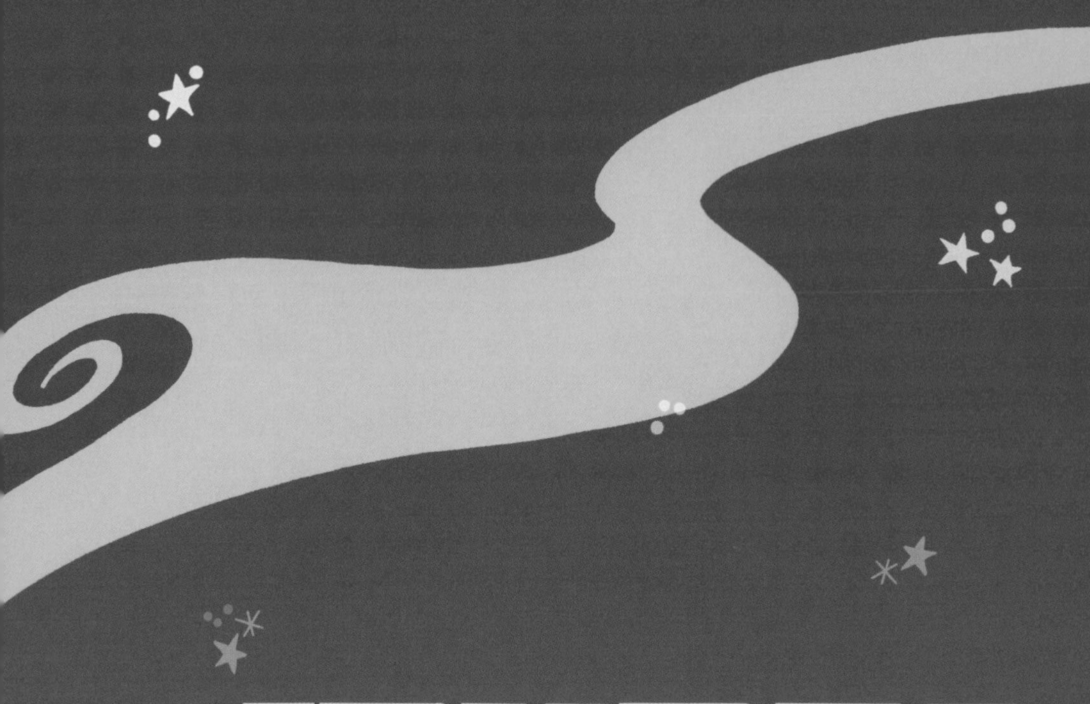

KRYPTO

The SUPERDOG™